MW01250561

# Niagara Falls

**Autumn Leigh**

Rosen
**REAL**
READERS

The Rosen Publishing Group, Inc.
New York

A waterfall is a stream of water that falls from a high place. Niagara Falls is one of the biggest waterfalls in the world!

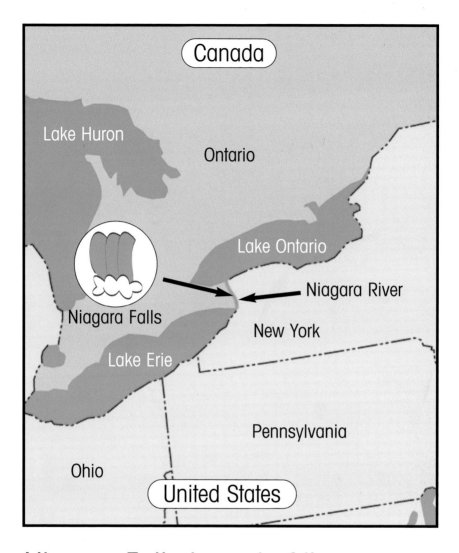

Niagara Falls is part of the
Niagara River. This river flows
between two of the **Great Lakes**,
from Lake Erie to Lake Ontario.

3

Ice covered this part of the world around 12,000 years ago. The Great Lakes and Niagara Falls formed when the ice **melted**.

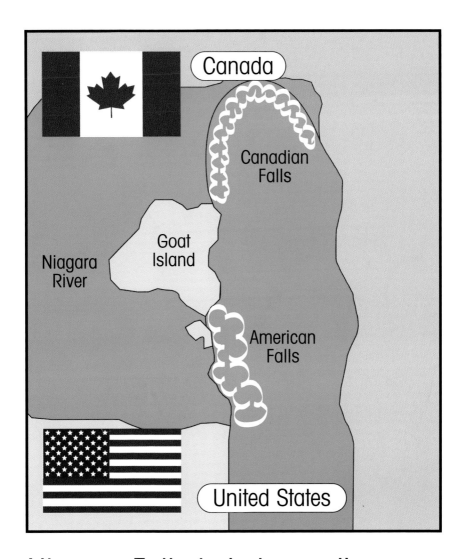

Niagara Falls is between the
United States and Canada.
These two countries share
Niagara Falls.

Niagara Falls is really two waterfalls. One waterfall is in the United States. The other waterfall is in Canada.

The American Falls is the taller waterfall. The American Falls is about 176 feet tall.

The Canadian waterfall is called the **Horseshoe** Falls. It is shaped like a horseshoe.

Goat Island

An **island** called Goat Island is between the American Falls and the Horseshoe Falls.

The water that goes over Niagara Falls is used to run **machines**. These machines make **power** for things we use, like lights.

About 10 million people come
from all over the world to see
Niagara Falls every year!

# Glossary

**Great Lakes**  Five large, freshwater lakes between the United States and Canada.

**horseshoe**  A piece of metal shaped like the letter U. The part of Niagara Falls in Canada is shaped like a horseshoe.

**island**  A piece of land that has water all around it.

**machine**  Something with moving parts that does work for people.

**melt**  To change ice into water by heating it.

**power**  A force that makes things work.